The *Innkeeper's Son*

KEN ANDERSON

The *Innkeeper's Son*

KEN ANDERSON

Merry Christmas
2006
Marion G. Baker

innovative
Christian Publications

Baker Trittin Press
Winona Lake, Indiana

Published by Innovative Christian Publications Division
Baker Trittin Press
P. O. Box 277
Winona Lake, Indiana 46590

The Innkeeper's Son
By Ken Anderson

To order additional copies please call 574-269-6100
or email info@btconcepts.com
http://www.gospelstoryteller.com

Publishers Cataloging- Publication Data
Anderson, Ken, 1917-
        The Innkeeper's Son /
        Ken Anderson - Winona Lake, Indiana: Baker Trittin Press

                p. cm.

Library of Congress Control Number: 2004110907
        ISBN: 0-9729256-9-4
        1. Fiction 2. Religious
        I. Title II. The Innkeeper's Son
FIC026000

Printed in the United States of America
Cover: Paul S. Trittin

to my children and grandchildren
all of whom have seen the light
and heard the song

the anthem
of that night
was not meant to be
words conveyed
or cadence intoned
but
lyric and melody
composed
and
rendered
in the heart
of anyone
for whom history's foremost moment
becomes contemporary

ka

CHAPTER ONE

On the night most remembered, the night when all the world began to change, the inn of the father of Elysmus was full beyond the taking of another taxpayer.

"By the names of all the prophets!" Bal Nahor cried out. He was flush from much wine and angered because his son complained about being moved from his usual sleeping place. "You eat the food my sweat provides! No boy of Bethlehem sits in finer robes at the feet of Arphaxad! But what thanks do I hear for the roof that cools you from the sun and shelters you from the rain? Asked to bear a small discomfort this night of your father's opportunity and you disgrace the blood of David flowing in your veins!"

Elysmus, standing beside his mother, watched a spider struggling across the cold stone floor.

The innkeeper lifted his wineskin and drank. He paused to emit a throaty belch and before taking another quaff brushed the half length of an arm across his reddened lips.

"Please, my husband!" Atarah, the man's wife, spoke with the respect required of Hebrew women. "Elysmus is a child. He is weary and, like both of us, he becomes impatient."

Bal Nahor responded by once more imbibing.

"Enough of the wine, my beloved husband," the woman ventured in soft-spoken reproof, "or you will be remiss in your duties!"

"How else am I to bear the weight of all my cares?" Bal Nahor defended. He drank again, more deeply than before.

Atarah stepped nearer a window overlooking the inn courtyard. Elysmus joined her. A late winter mist descended, visibly back-lighted by a sheltered torch.

"Again the sky weeps," Atarah said, sighing. "When it remained dry through the morning, my heart rejoiced for the many travelers. One wishes the inn could shelter every stranger who sojourns to Bethlehem. How dare we leave anyone to the night's chill?

"We refuse any who cannot pay my price!" the innkeeper replied. He cursed. "Would I had begun charging higher fees before sundown and had a hundred rooms to swell the coffer. Half-blind and half-fool my father was . . . setting his business in the miserable poverty of Bethlehem! Better far somewhere like Jerusalem!"

"How many inns must there be in Jerusalem?" Atarah asked.

Bal Nahor gave no reply. With one hand he smoothed his cloak and tunic, with the other he lifted the wineskin.

"At this late time of the season," Atarah said, "fortunately the rain falls mostly by intervals. It appears to be lessening now."

She sighed.

"May there be no one traveling who is ill or in need of warmth."

She took a brave step toward her husband.

"The second watch has been called," she said. "You have given our quarters to the shipbuilder from Ashkelon." She remained silent while her husband partook of more wine. Then, cautiously, she added, "You say the two of us are to take the boy's nook. So where, pray tell, shall Elysmus sleep?"

"Abasing flaw from my loins, that boy," Bal Nahor scoffed. "What good can ever be made of him?"

"Too much wine defiles the lips of the best among men," Atarah countered bravely. "Our son is one of the boys most praised by the lips of Arphaxad, the great teacher. Elysmus is skilled in the *Mishna* and has advanced above the others in the first teachings of the *Talmud*. We know, both of us, how Arphaxad expects students to be most diligent in the sacred scrolls. How many of the writings our son holds treasured in his memory!" A smile touched her countenance. "What joy it is when he recites them for us!"

The innkeeper scoffed and asked, "Become a bearer for the temple, shall he? Live off alms as beggars do?"

"Arphaxad has told us our son could become one of the most learned of the Pharisees," Atarah countered. "Think how proud we would be at festival time to see Elysmus . . . "

"A good deal prouder if he were one of the Sadducees," Bal Nahor interrupted, "his pockets jingling with Caesar's coins."

"Elysmus is destined for a noble future," Atarah assured. In a near-whisper, she added, "He could be an awaited prophet!"

"Prophet?" Bal Nahor spoke in that moment as if he were sober. "Jehovah's lips have been sealed four hundred years. I've heard men at the gate say we should all worship Caesar and be done with Roman oppression. Jehovah? A man was crucified within this fortnight for daring to quote Levitical law to one of the centurions. Arphaxad himself some morning soon may carry a cross up one of the hills."

"My husband!" Atarah cried out. "Guard your lips!"

"I speak the truth!" her husband countered. "A man would as wisely enter the temple wearing a saharonim of Roman design as to bedeck himself with our Hebrew phylacteries."

The two remained silent for a time. Atarah took her husband's vine wood staff from its niche on the wall, dusted it lightly with her apron as if to appease the man. Elysmus looked out the window, out into the darkness, upward toward the sky where small fissures in the cloud-cover permitted the faint glimmer of what the boy assumed to be the moon. He turned his eyes onto the surrounding area, saw the last light from a far window extinguished, leaving all of visible Bethlehem hushed and dark.

Elysmus heard his mother saying, "Pray tell me, where shall your son sleep tonight?"

"Let him bed with the animals!"

"Bal Nahor!" Atarah exclaimed. "However despitefully you speak now of Elysmus, you yourself said a moment ago he has the lineage of David in his veins!" She watched in silence as her husband continued his drinking. Then, venturing cautiously, she asked, "What words might men at the gate speak if they learned of such shamefulness . . . our son, asleep in the straw and the dung?"

"My friends at the gate will want to know what weight of shekels I have gained from this time of prosperity. "They . . ." Bal Nahor drank again. "They will press me to toss dice onto the gaming board," he continued, "and dare a poor innkeeper to wager more than his purse has made possible!"

Atarah touched her son's shoulder moving him away.

"We will find a place for you to sleep," she told him. Beyond her husband's hearing, she added, "We must be of least trouble to your father. Tonight is like no other night. Not since the last counting of the people has little Bethlehem known the footsteps of so many strangers."

"Father dislikes me," Elysmus said with sadness.

"Your father dislikes everyone," Atarah replied. ". . . the more so when leavened nectar sets a torch to his head."

Mother and son came to the chamber where the stores were kept. It was full of provisions brought in for these days of the census, bags and baskets, wooden casks of vinegar, earthen containers of parched corn. The pleasant smell of last harvest's wheat wafted toward the doorway. There were earthen casks of honey, goatskins taut with fermented wine.

"If I can think of no other," Atarah said, "we can perhaps move items about and fix you a space here."

"In the stores room, Mother?" Elysmus pouted softly. "Scorpions pass through. I once saw a lizard. There are mice. There could be rats."

"I say you would sleep here only if your mother cannot think of a better place." Woman and boy faced each other briefly. Atarah clutched an embroidered corner of her headdress and pressed it to her lower lip. "O my son, thank the Lord Jehovah you are too young to understand the tumult of this night."

Atarah took a terracotta lamp from a ledge nearby and lifted it to survey the contents of the stores room.

"We could perhaps find a comfortable place," she said.

She turned back the first fold of a camel's hair rug and acrid dust wafted across the enclosure.

"But the scorpions!" the boy protested.

"*Once* we destroyed a scorpion, Elysmus . . . only once. That was seasons ago."

"The mice and rats, Mother!"

"They are as shy of you as you of them."

Atarah gestured against her son's further complaint.

"Tell me of the day," she said with motherly gentleness. "We have been so hurried here at the inn I have not asked you about your studies. What did you learn this day from the wise lips of Arphaxad?"

Elysmus continued his pouting and his silence.

"Come! Come! Scrolls and learning are ever so much more important than scorpions and mice!"

The boy parted his lips but did not speak.

"Please, Elysmus," the mother prodded. "I have told you this is like no other night. Fate affords you opportunity to be helpful rather than hindering. Remember the scrolls of Nehemiah, how the people worked as one rebuilding Jerusalem's walls? Without murmuring . . . fathers and mothers . . . children as well."

When her son's silence continued, his mother said, "Arphaxad himself bids you keep always in your heart Commandment Five from the tablets given to Moses."

Elysmus turned away. His mother turned him back so the two again faced each other.

"Recite that commandment for me . . . Commandment Five . . . as you have so often done!" There was no warmth in his mother's voice. There was sternness in her eyes.

"Recite, Elysmus!"

"Honor your father and your mother," the boy repeated by rote, "that your days may be long upon the land."

"The very words of Jehovah!" Atarah exclaimed while giving her son a hasty embrace. "Now tell me of today's classes," she continued, busying herself with stored items. "What did you hear from the lips of the venerable teacher?"

Elysmus yawned.

"Tell me, Elysmus! What we learn of Jehovah's ways is ever more important than our earthly needs."

"Our teacher reads each day from the scrolls of Isaiah," the boy began. "Some days his eyes fail him. Then he asks one of us to read. In these recent days, a servant has led him to the synagogue and returned him to his home."

"Have you shared your eyes with Arphaxad?"

"Yes, Mother."

"You have held the scrolls?" Atarah gasped. "You have read as do the teachers and the priests?"

"I have."

"Honor upon honor! Surely you will one day be a leader among our people!" The mother placed a loving hand upon her son's shoulder. "You have read from the scrolls of Isaiah?"

"Often," Elysmus replied.

"The very scrolls of Isaiah! O my gifted child, no Sabbath readings so please your mother's ears as do the prophesies of Isaiah! Tell on! What does the respected one teach you about the greatest among the prophets?"

"Arphaxad wept this day as he told us he surely will not walk the valley of death before Messiah's coming."

Atarah was so startled by her son's words she would have

dropped a small cask of honey had not Elysmus reached out quickly to sustain it in her hands.

"Tell me more!" she urged.

"David's seed will flourish," Elysmus began.

"Yes?"

"Gold will fall from the skies as did manna in the wilderness."

"Ah!" Atarah sang out. "Even your wayward father will consecrate himself to Jehovah's service!" She moved items about to prepare a sleeping place. "You could if needed sleep on these grain skins," she said. She glanced at her son and, in the same breath, urged, "Speak further about Arphaxad's teaching this day!"

"He read from many of the scrolls," the boy said. "He reads, as to himself, and we boys do not hear many of the words."

"An old, old man is Arphaxad," the woman said kindly, "yet he could be Elijah returned to earth again. Would that all men in Judea shared the richness of his soul." She grew pensive as she continued, "Does he speak further about the prophecy from the scroll of the Prophet Micah?"

"He has told us nothing more," the boy replied. While his mother stood in quiet thought, he said cautiously, "Surely I cannot sleep here. Let me do as Father said, and. . . ."

"One more time!" Atarah interrupted. "Recite again the words of the Prophet Micah!"

Elysmus kept silent. Surely he had recited the words to her twice the counting of his fingers. More if numbering the times when, with patrons few and his wine supply drunk away, Bal Nahor himself listened to the rendering.

"I wish to sleep, Mother," the boy complained. "It is far

into the second watch."

"Your mother knows, dear child, but reciting the scriptures can rest you more than sleep."

"Perhaps tomorrow . . ."

"Elysmus!" Atarah demanded in a sudden change of temperament. "The writings of the Prophet!"

Elysmus wished to delay further, but such a look of displeasure came to his mother's eyes he stepped to his full height, placed his arms straight and properly at his sides and began reciting from the prophet Micah. "Bethlehem Ephrathah, though you are little among the thousands of Judah, yet out of you shall come forth to Me the One to be Ruler in Israel."

Atarah dropped to her knees. She held the lamp close to her son's face. The sternness of her countenance gave place to the sheen of a mother's pride.

"From the lips of my own bearing," she exclaimed, "the prophecies of the Promised One! O Elysmus! Speak the words another time that the lowly woman who bore you may listen in closeness to your blessed voice."

Elysmus complied. His mother formed the words silently with the speaking of her son, retreating thereafter into such a time of reverie the boy supposed she had forgotten about his need for a sleeping place.

"When Messiah comes, all shall prosper," Atarah mused. "He will set us free from our oppressors. As happened to Pharaoh's armies at the Red Sea, the soldiers of Rome shall be destroyed."

Doing a small dance at the entrance to the stores chamber, she sang out, "In majesty He will come! King of all Kings! Lord of all Lords! Greater than ever was Solomon, or the whole of the prophets and priests and kings of all time."

CHAPTER TWO

Elysmus had never seen his mother in such display. Although he neither understood nor shared her ecstasy, he saw this altered mood as his own time of opportunity.

"The stores chamber is very full, Mother," he said cautiously. "Could I bed in the stable? With the animals as father himself said? Please, Mother? The sheep would welcome me! They know me as they know themselves!'

Atarah's countenance was once again troubled. Elysmus presumed this to be the result of his request.

"The prophet's words," Atarah said slowly, hesitating.

Must he quote them yet another time? the boy wondered.

"If Messiah shall arise from Bethlehem," Atarah continued, "does Arphaxad say He will descend from heaven to our little town?"

Elysmus did not respond.

"Might Messiah even now be born in Bethlehem does Arphaxad say? But whose dwelling is noble enough? Surely not within the walls of Herod's evil. . . . "

She paused, her mouth open but void of speech. She put

out her hand and touched her son, and she looked into his eyes as if expecting him to speak further of the hoped for advent.

"I do remember . . ." the boy began.

"More of Arphaxad's teaching?" Atarah questioned. "Tell your mother!"

"Our teacher has placed many of the prophet Isaiah's writings into our memories," Elysmus said.

"About Bethlehem?" Atarah asked.

"About Messiah."

"Recite such words to your mother! O yes, my son! Do!"

Elysmus formed his lips for speech as his mind searched to remember. Then, to his astonishment, the words of Isaiah came clearly to his thoughts.

"The Lord Himself will give you a sign," he recited slowly.

When he paused for clearer reflection, his mother urged, "Continue, my son, my own blessed of Jehovah."

"A sign . . ." the boy continued searching for words.

"A sign," his mother repeated.

"The virgin shall conceive and . . ."

"And. . . ." Atarah prompted. She stroked her son's hand.

"And bear a Son," Elysmus remembered, "and shall call His name Immanuel."

"Immanuel! The Messiah!" Atarah exclaimed. "God with us." She embraced her son and exclaimed with delight, "You have been given the heart of a patriarch. Samuel in the temple, in his service to Eli, was in mind and manner like unto my own son! Tell me, Elysmus. . . ."

"Out! Out! Out!" Bal Nahor's trumpeting voice interrupted from the inner chambers.

Startled, Atarah looked away, her words cut off by her

husband's outburst.

In the next moment, the burly innkeeper lumbered past the stores room doorway pushing the half-asleep man from Ashkelon whom he had lifted out of the sleeping place allotted to him for the night.

"I paid for my lodging!" the man was heard protesting as he struggled against being thrust toward the outer doorway. "I paid three times your usual price!"

Mother and son ventured into a hidden view of the courtyard. They watched as Bal Nahor, holding the evicted guest securely, stepped onto the cobbled courtyard. A nobleman and his wife and children stood waiting. Servants tended the camels of their caravan.

"Shall you wish to lodge your animals in my stable?" Bal Nahor asked. His voice resembled that of a sober man.

"No need," replied the patrician. "They have slept in the night air beside our tents since Sidon. A strange stable would turn them skittish."

Meanwhile, the shipbuilder, now awakened more fully, had wrested himself free of Bal Nahor's grasp. He attempted to return into the building.

"I go back to my sleep place," he defied.

Bal Nahor blocked his way, asking, "When have you, until tonight, sought rest beneath my roof?" The innkeeper gestured to the nobleman. "This patrician comes each year at the last of the harvest, he and a caravan of merchants, at which time they pay me handsomely for the whole of my inn. What sort of ingrate would I be to deny him and his family this night?"

"I claim no less prominence!" the deposed boarder exclaimed. "Ships built by myself and my artisans sail to Puteoli and Athens, to Carthage and Byzantium."

"Sail on, stranger," Bal Nahor bellowed. "Not a splash from your ship's hull has ever fallen on me. So be gone!"

"Where am I to go?" the man asked.

"Go to the town center," replied Bal Nahor with a wave of his hand, "where multitudes like you spend this night around their warming fires."

The innkeeper took coins from his pocket and sorted out the amount the man had previously paid.

"Hire a night of Megira's services. She shares her bed with anyone who pays the price." Bal Nahor laughed as he forced the coins into the shipbuilder's hand. "Here and be on with you."

He then escorted the man to the courtyard entrance, there pushing him out into the darkness.

Elysmus looked up at his mother, seeing her in the light cast from the torches at the inn entrance.

"It is forbidden to send a guest away," Atarah whispered.

"I regret causing you inconvenience," the nobleman was heard to say. "I shall speak of you at many a city gate in the course of my often journeys."

Bal Nahor came now toward the inn. Atarah grasped her son's arm and moved both of them back to the stores room. There the innkeeper met them.

"Ah, yes! The stores," he exclaimed. "A clever woman despite your many failings. You have made a bed for us among the stores."

His pleasure was short-lived.

"Quick, woman," he commanded, "prepare the two rooms."

"Two rooms?"

"The nobleman and his wife will sleep where we had

placed the shipbuilder, and the nobleman's children will have our son's chamber."

"Our son's chamber?" Atarah asked cautiously. "You said it was to be for us."

"Do as I say, woman!"

"Where will we sleep?" Atarah wanted to know.

"Here in the stores room," her husband replied. "Now hurry."

"And Elysmus? What of him?"

Bal Nahor hesitated a moment. "Our son will go to the stable and sleep with the animals," he said.

Not waiting for his mother's comment, Elysmus darted away, out the entrance, off toward the stable cave a stone's toss from the inn.

As Elysmus paused at the entrance to the stable cave, the scent of animals, their forage and dung droppings, wafted upward into the night's wet chill. The scuff of his first footfall evoked an alarmed cry from a new-born lamb. Elysmus whistled softly, and recognizing, the mother ewe bleated reassurance to her youngling.

"She knows it is I." the boy proudly told himself.

He understood with what displeasure his mother and father looked upon his love for the animals. In spite of frequent insults and demeanings, Bal Nahor was known at the gate to be the father who boasted of his son's reputation as a student of the esteemed Arphaxad. Ofttimes, when sober, the slow-witted innkeeper listened without comment as his wife spoke of their son one day becoming a man of prominence, whether merchant or minister. As for Elysmus, he fancied a shepherd's life . . . guiding his flock by day, guarding them against leopards and jackals that prowled the night's darkness. This he never told his mother and father since shepherds had come to such low reputation in Israel.

"Night robbers they are," the boy's mother warned. "They will kill both to protect their sheep and to steal a journeying man's possessions."

Arphaxad had explained to his students about Migdal Eder, the sacred tower outside Bethlehem which overlooked the grazing lands of flocks kept for sacrificial purposes in the temple at Jerusalem.

"The herdsmen who tend the sheep at Migdal Eder are like the people everywhere," Arphaxad said. "It is of them Hosea wrote, 'Jehovah will reject them because they have not obeyed Him'"

And so, despite his love of the flocks, Elysmus could not rid himself of fearing the shepherds. He hid himself when they came near the inn and moved quickly out of sight if ever he saw them elsewhere in Bethlehem. But, secure in the confines of the inn compound, he had no thoughts of such or any other dangers as, pausing at the entrance to the stable cave, he looked up at the sky, leaden with cloud-cover. At the apex, a strange brightness had formed; the moon's effort to pierce through the boy supposed.

Arphaxad was a man of continuing sadness. "The Shekinah has been withdrawn to the Seventh Heaven," he lamented. "Only the intercession of the angels prevents earth and sky from being destroyed during this long delay of Messiah's coming."

Yet the old and honored rabbi had also taught his young learners many of the wonders of the earth and the heavens. He was skilled in the knowledge of the Egyptians. He quoted freely from the scrolls of Ptolemy, the Greek astronomer whose calculations of the heavens and the bright star Sirus confounded the wonder of those who slept by day so they could devote night hours to mysteries overhead.

"As our enslaved forbears must have known," the old man told his students, "each appearance of the bright star Sirus summons the rising waters of the great river Nile, enriching the land of Egypt horizon upon horizon. Who can tell what is yet to be learned of the heavenly lights and the measure of their relationship to our earth and our lives? The ancient Chaldeans, albeit their masterful astronomy, were but babes compared to what we will yet behold of Jehovah's handiwork."

Often, to the delight of boys like Elysmus, Arphaxad spoke more about the earth and the sky than he did of the sacred scrolls themselves.

At the teacher's command one day, Elysmus read from David's writing, "The heavens declare the glory of God; and the firmament shows his handiwork. Day unto day utters speech. And night unto night reveals knowledge."

"Enough! Enough!" the old man cried out curtly.

Then his eyes, like minute stars, gazed out above his students as he spoke of heavenly bodies.

Aries, the Lamb.

Bethulah, the Virgin.

Libra's gigantic cross in the southern skies.

"We have yet to learn the meaning of these wonders," was all he could say in explanation.

"Soon Messiah will come," he said one recent day. "Who knows what songs birds will then sing? What flowers may burst into first bloom? What amazements the heavens will display? Egypt and Babylon, Athens and Rome, they shall be as wilderness camps when shadowed by the majesty of Messiah's advent."

The distant bleat of his cherished ewe emerged through the darkness causing Elysmus to look away from the sky.

"I am your shepherd," the boy sang out, "and I am coming."

Imitating the sound of a lyre, to harmonize a melody he had learned at synagogue lessons, Elysmus imagined himself a guard in Messiah's court as he walked sure of step down the incline and into the darkness of the cave. He knew the stable in its every detail, for he came often, and proceeded directly toward the manger and stall of his favorite ewe. She had within that fortnight dropped two lambs in thorn-bush shade a scant furlong from the inn sheepfold. Elysmus himself gathered them into his arms and, the ewe following, toted them back to the stable.

In one moment's hand search, he came upon the manger site, a hewn indentation into the cave's rough rock outer wall which he imagined to be like a burial nook in one of the sepulchers he had heard his parents describe.

By the scanning of his hands, he came upon the ewe with the newborns nestled against her underside.

The pleased animal nuzzled him.

He scratched above her ears.

David had been a shepherd. The thought came often to the boy's mind. At times, when watching his father's small flock in fields adjacent to Bethlehem, he pretended himself to be the long honored singer and king. One day, at rest upon a jutting thrust of limestone, he thought to write a psalm of his own.

"Jehovah! Great Jehovah!" he pretended to inscribe upon a fragment of cedar bark. "The sky is Thine! The sun and the moon are Thine. The hills and the valleys and all the birds and creatures. . . ." Here he had paused, quite swept up in the novelty of the experience. Then he lifted the cedar bark and added, "All shepherd boys are also Thine, O Great Jehovah."

He recited the origination to his mother. At first, in her customary manner, she praised her son. Soon after she became apprehensive, however, and said, "Take care lest it be shameful and unrighteous to think such as you could add to the holy writings."

After thus speaking, she stood a long moment looking at her son. Slowly the reprimanding cast upon her countenance gave place to an expression of questioning wonder.

"No prophet has spoken in four hundred years," she had said quietly, turning away to attend some household chores. She abruptly turned back to add, "When you were born and bathed and I looked fully upon you, you were so beautiful I sinned in thinking you might be Shiloh, the Promised One."

Having said that, she walked briskly to another room.

Here in the stable, although he thought of his composition and remembered his mother's strange reaction, Elysmus recited another of the Messiah passages from Isaiah which Arphaxad had taught his students. "He will feed His flock like a shepherd; He will gather the lambs with His arms and carry them in His bosom."

Touching the mother ewe, he remembered how, at the last Passover, his own tears protested his father's drunken scheme of bringing this, the finest of their flock, to the atonement altar.

"The scrolls teach that ewes are not suitable for sacrifices," Elysmus had sobbed to his mother. "Please tell Father only males are to be brought."

"Have you so completely forgotten your own learning as

a boy?" Atarah chided her husband.

Bal Nahor, although a man of meager piety, would have by reason of his surly nature ignored the words of his wife and son. He had taken on a full measure of wine and thus incorrectly selected a female from the flock.

"He cares but little for the sacrifice itself," Atarah had quietly told her son. "He wishes the finest of the flock to gain the nodding of men at the gate."

To her husband, with boldness uncustomary for a Hebrew wife, she said, "Elysmus has spared us the foolishness and shame of coming to the altar with an improper offering. What make of Jew would you be, my husband, ignorant of disobeying the most elementary teachings?"

Bal Nahor then reached for his wineskin. Finding it empty, he tossed it aside.

Of their son, Atarah said, "Each time he returns from studies at the synagogue, Elysmus brings me the words of Arphaxad. The teacher believes the Messiah may soon come. We will from that time onward bring no sacrifices to the altar."

So it came to be that Bal Nahor chose a young male lamb for the Passover oblation.

With a prayer learned at synagogue, Elysmus had whispered heavenward: "Give thanks to the Lord, for He is good." Gratitude now aglow in his heart as he remembered the frightening experience, the boy moved closely against the warmth of his animal friend and drowsed to the first point of sleep, humming the melody of one of his favorite songs. "The Lord is my shepherd, I shall not want."

Shepherd?

He sat up wondering.

Might Messiah come as a man of the flocks and the fields? Not as a mighty king? Not in the splendor as his teacher said? Such thoughts had never before appeared in the boy's mind. Were they evil?

From the writings of King Solomon, Arphaxad had one day read, "The thoughts of the wicked are an abomination to the Lord."

Troubled, as he lay back, Elysmus tossed upon the straw, disturbing the ewe that turned to an alternate position.

"Elsymus!"

The boy sat up in fear. The figure of a woman, dimly lighted by the flame of a small lamp she carried, came toward him.

"I repent for my thoughts," he cried out.

He then saw that the woman was his mother. She carried his outer cloak across her arm.

"Whatever are you saying?" she asked.

Elysmus did not reply.

Atarah came to her son and leaned forward to touch his shoulder and beckon him from his comfort beside the ewe.

"You must not sleep here," she said.

"It was Father's command," the boy countered.

"Your father's stomach is a wineskin this night. He spoke with the lips of a fool telling you to bed with the animals. Now come, for I have a thought."

Elysmus turned himself and proceeded to crawl across the manger.

"You are one of the favored students of Arphaxad." Atarah spoke with caution. "Like the child Samuel of old, can we say?"

The boy came alongside his mother.

"Such were your great teacher's words to your father and me at the synagogue on a recent Sabbath."

"Our teacher praises other boys as well," Elysmus replied modestly.

"If you went to his dwelling, even at this late hour," Atarah continued, "if you explained the turmoil at the inn, would not Arphaxad give you a place to sleep?"

She opened the boy's cloak and placed it across his shoulders.

"The night's wetness forbids anyone's passage," she said, "but, as I have told you, this is like no other night."

Elysmus was at first startled. How could he, a mere boy, approach the residence of the revered Arphaxad even by full day? From this late watch, how dare he ever think of entering the respected dwelling?

"Your mother will see you there safely."

Atarah's words quieted her son's apprehension. He looked back at the ewe and the lambs. Comfortable though it had been lying with them, the thought of a night's lodging in the home of his teacher aroused his interest.

The two moved toward the stable egress. The lamp light frightened a dove. It fluttered to another roosting site. Had there been daylight, it likely would have perched upon the boy's shoulder, for it often took food from his hand.

"I dare not send you alone to ask your teacher's favor," the mother said. "One must pass through town center. Who knows what evil occurs there with so many drunken strangers in Bethlehem's darkness?" She sighed. "Were it not for the inn, your father would be among the revelers."

As they approached the cave's outer opening, Atarah

cautioned, "Let us guard our steps in this wetness."

Elysmus did not hear his mother's speaking for an astonishing wonder occurred. Mid-day light burst through an opening in the sky as though a thousand torches had been lit against the night.

The boy looked to his mother, her face faintly illumined by the flickering of her lamp. She seemed unaware of the sky. Her son held up his hand made bright by the descending brilliance.

"Bethlehem's streets will be very dark at this hour," Atarah said, "but we will make our way carefully."

Scarcely hearing, the boy hurried up the rock-hewn incline for full view. Mist, falling steadily, was becoming akin to soft rainfall. Yet, in the sky directly above, one lone star had broken through the overcast to shine downward as though clouds had been banished from the sky.

"O Mother," Elysmus cried, "the clouds have opened!"

Atarah came alongside her son and paused, glancing at the sky. Rain drops fell lightly, and she lifted her shawl for shelter. A quick wind sweep blew out her lamp flame. "This is no time for fantasies, Elysmus," she said brusquely.

"There is a new star!" Elysmus exclaimed. "See how very bright it is? Brighter than the moon would be. Brighter than I have ever seen before! Is it. . . ? "

Just then the voice of Bal Nahor sounded out in drunken loudness from the inn courtyard.

"There is no room! Be you David's blood or Caesar's. This is a small inn, and I could have let for the night three times our fullest occupancy."

Atarah looked toward the inn.

"How big the star is!" Elysmus exclaimed as he returned to his mother's side. "How bright!"

He touched Atarah's arm and pointed to the sky. She did not respond. Her attention was upon the courtyard where a man stood with a haltered donkey. A woman sat on the animal.

"The rain," the man said. He motioned toward his wife. "We must find shelter."

"Go to Herod's palace," the innkeeper called out in drunken jest. "Tell the guards your soon born is the next Jewish king. Like as not, they are no less drunk than I am."

"The star," Elysmus once more said to his mother.

She moved forward into the rainy space between the stable and the inn entrance. The boy looked about him. He saw himself in a large circle of light. His mother moved forward through the night's darkness.

What could the meaning be?

Was he yet asleep beside the ewe, asleep and dreaming?

"I am Joseph, a carpenter from Nazareth," Elysmus heard the man say. "It has been a journey of three days."

"I tell you," Bal Nahor retorted, "you could be Augustus from Rome or the King of Cappadocia and my words would be unchanged. There is no room!"

The man named Joseph saw Atarah approaching.

"The breath of Jehovah is upon my wife," he called to her. "It is her first bearing. We must find shelter!"

Elysmus turned away from the sky and moved into the courtyard.

"O Joseph," the woman cried out, "it will be soon!"

Stepping next to his mother, Elysmus saw an instant's compassion in her eyes. He also saw the light of the star fell fully upon the man and the woman from Nazareth.

But not upon either of his parents.

Far into the distance, beyond the shepherd's fields, a peal of thunder sounded. At the same moment, the rain increased its intensity.

Feigning cordiality, Bal Nahor patted the carpenter's shoulder. "Jehovah is thy shepherd, King David wrote, something to that effect. Without Jehovah's wisdom and bestowal, there could not be wombs or babies, could there? He will see you through the night."

Then the innkeeper stumbled toward the inn.

"Please, good friend," the man called out.

Bal Nahor did not look back.

"From Nazareth I come, I come." The innkeeper sang and laughed. He attempted to imitate itinerant minstrels who always depicted Nazarenes with the dialect of the herdsman along the plains of Esdraelon. "You have for sleep my wife and me a bed?" the innkeeper continued. He uttered a blatant vulgarity, adding, "What one good thing has ever come from Nazareth?"

Atarah came into view.

"Can you show us mercy?" Joseph pled.

"I. . . ." Atarah replied, hesitating. She reached out to the woman seated upon the donkey. Then she turned away, and as she walked briskly toward the inn she added, "I must find a resting place for our son. Come, Elysmus, we will put on warmer clothing and hasten to the dwelling of your teacher."

As Elysmus moved away to follow his mother, Joseph's hand took firm hold of the boy's arm, restraining him.

"What is that opening I see in the starlight?" Joseph asked.

"Our stable cave," the boy replied.

"Quickly," the man gently commanded, "fetch water to the stable."

Elysmus hesitated, looking up to his mother for approval. Atarah who had paused waiting for her son stood in silent uneasiness.

"Be what help you can," she said. She turned and continued with uncertainty toward the inn, glancing back to say to her son, "Perhaps I can yet find a place for you inside."

"If there is a place," Elysmus called to his mother, "it could be for these people. I would go to the house of Arphaxad."

Atarah gave no response.

Elysmus looked up once more at the sky. Unaffected by the mist and rain, the new star had become like a fragment of the sun, causing the cave entrance to appear as if it were in daylight compared to the surrounding darkness.

"Hurry, dear boy," the carpenter from Nazareth urged. "Bring a basin of water and a flagon of salt."

Elysmus ran to the inn.

The man led his donkey toward the cave entrance.

CHAPTER THREE

In his haste to be helpful, Elysmus took from the inn a bronze chalice used only at Passover time and when his parents called at the temple. An heirloom handed down from Atarah's forebears, the sacred vessel lay overturned atop an oil cask in the cooking sector. Bal Nahor had taken it from the nearby chest of family treasures, thinking to serve wine to an afternoon customer of lucrative potential. Only when his wife restrained him from committing such sacrilege did the innkeeper, grumbling dissent, put the item down.

In his excitement, Elysmus did not think of the chalice's seldom yet sacred function. As he took a small cut of linen to dust the bowl, his father entered. Elysmus turned to his father in fear, but the drunken man gave no notice except to push his son aside.

Bal Nahor slumped onto the family chest which he had once taken in trade from a Nazareth lodger. It was of wooden construction, small in measure, and sitting upon it he could pour the contents of his money bag onto the floor.

"*Echad, shahaim, shalosh, arba-ah,*" he counted the coins,

singing out each numeral like a troubadour at the city gate.

Elysmus was placing the cloth back where he had found it when his mother appeared. She saw her son only in a glance, her attention coming fully on her husband.

"Bal Nahor! Be not a fool," Atarah scolded, boldly outspoken because of her husband's drunkenness. "Thieves are everywhere in Bethlehem tonight. Even a drunken shepherd will know an innkeeper receives many weights of money at such a time."

She moved impulsively to a wall niche to snatch away a lamp flickering from the last of its oil. She slapped her hand over the flame stifling it and sending the room into darkness.

"Light!" Bal Nahor bellowed. "I need light!"

"You need to think more than you need to see." Atarah retorted and with those words she was gone.

Although the area of the inn from which he now departed lay in darkness and although the rain persisted, Elysmus approached the watering place encircled by the star's silvery brightness. As he lifted the chalice to receive its fill of water, the star's light turned the bronze color of the vessel into a purple hue . . . like the garments rich men wore, like priestly robes at the temple. The effect gave Elysmus both a moment's fright and the first realization he had taken a treasured item no hands so young as his should ever touch.

He must return the chalice to the inn with fullest haste. But there was the need at the stable cave. As though prompted by an inner voice, he felt compelled to answer that need. He must take whatever might be the consequences of his mistake. So he lifted the chalice and hurried on his way.

The consciousness of wrong became like a knife at his

heart. He remembered the lessons from 1 Chronicles that Arphaxad had given about the sanctity of sacred things. Uzzah, on the threshing floor of Kidon, only had touched the Ark of the Covenant to steady it from falling and was smitten dead by Jehovah.

Surely the anger of his father would be great when, sobered from the night's wine, he learned that the most sacred of the family's possessions had been used for an unclean purpose. How much more then might be Jehovah's displeasure?

Elysmus would have returned to the inn except that, as he looked toward the cave entrance, he witnessed a new phenomenon. Brighter than from the sky overhead, brighter than the sun at noonday, abounding light flowed out from the stable's interior. And, as if swept up from within by that billowing brightness, a figure appeared. This figure was not so much illuminated by the light as being part of the light itself.

The boy stood silent, watching.

"Angel!" he whispered instinctively.

He was so aroused by the spectacle, he let the chalice slip from his hands.

Or so he thought.

To his amazement, the chalice reappeared in the angel's hands!

"This is the night foretold by the prophets," the angel declared. "Go and make known."

Having spoken those commands, the figure disappeared. So also did the chalice.

Elysmus stood for a long moment so stunned he nearly fell to the ground.

Foretold?

Prophets?

What were the meanings of such words? How could a young boy understand? How might he know the event had happened or if he was having the most amazing dream of his life?

He swung his arms.

He jumped into the air.

Once.

Twice.

Again and more.

He remembered such actions as the culmination of strange dreams he had experienced and, having now repeated the motions, anticipated awakening.

But he did not awaken for, as he dared to believe, this was no dream. It was as real as when Samuel, lying awake in the temple, was visited by Jehovah.

Elysmus looked again to the sky. Rainfall subsided. Cloud-cover remained, except a fissure overhead from which descended the brightness of the wonderful star!

Then, simultaneously from the heavens and from the stable came singing beyond the beauty of anything his ears had past times known.

"Glory to God in the highest!"

Louder and louder the voices resounded like a celestial pronouncement, yet sweet and singular as though the melody were composed and rendered from the deeps of his own heart.

In that moment, one word came to his lips. He uttered the word in the awe of its majesty but also in fear, wondering if, like the chalice, the word was not his to employ.

"Messiah!"

Ever more loudly, the singing!

Ever brighter and glorious the descending light!

"Messiah! Messiah!"

Elysmus became bold beyond himself as each utterance filled him with abounding wonder and with an anointing that penetrated to the marrow.

Yet, questions came to his mind.

How could it be?

In a stable cave?

"Glory to God in the highest, and on earth peace good will toward men."

The singing plummeted down upon him, engulfed him, as though in response to his uncertainty.

With his fullest strength he ran toward the inn.

"Mother!" he cried. "See! Hear!"

Atarah met him at the entrance.

"What is wrong?" his mother wanted to know, taking him into light embrace. "Have thieves come to the stable?"

Wrestling partly free, Elysmus pointed to the star.

"See!" he exclaimed. "In the sky!"

"What am I to see?"

"The star, Mother! The sky is full of clouds but see how it opens for the star?"

Atarah looked and said, "I see no star."

"And the singing, Mother . . . do you hear. . . ."

"Elysmus!" Atarah now took full grasp of her son and shook him soundly. "You are taken with madness."

"Messiah has come!" the boy exclaimed, "to our stable, Mother! Hear the singing? Messiah! I saw the. . . ."

Atarah cupped her hand forcefully across her son's mouth.

"Blasphemy!" she cried out. "Bal Nahor! My husband!"

The innkeeper came staggering. He grasped his wife's arm, pulling her so abruptly she lost hold of Elysmus.

"Fool, woman!" Bal Nahor rent the night air with a curse. "Disturb the sleep of our patrons? Is it such folly to you, your husband knowing these few hours of prosperity?"

Standing free, Elysmus looked up at the star. Its brightness caught him full in the face. He held up his hand and saw the brightness reflected upon his flesh.

And, on and on, the singing.

He looked to his parents. No light fell upon them. They seemed to hear nothing but their tirades against each other.

"Arphaxad," Elysmus uttered.

Yes, he must tell Arphaxad.

"Where do you go?" he heard his mother calling as he scurried out of the courtyard.

"To the house of my teacher," Elysmus called back.

"Wait!" Atarah exclaimed. "I go with you."

She lunged forward but Bal Nahor restrained her. Holding her firmly, the innkeeper put aside his harshness with a pretense of piety and affection.

"We shall end this day of Jehovah's abundance by going to our bed!" he told his wife as he drew her with him to the inn.

CHAPTER FOUR

With bursts of boyhood fitness, Elysmus bounded away from the inn, off across a small clearing and onto narrow Bethlehem streets toward the town center, the synagogue and house of Arphaxad, his teacher. Rain and mist no longer fell. The Advent Star lighted his pathway with an escorting circle. Around him, like the antiphonal rendering of a Psalm in temple services, angel voices sang from one point on the horizon, *Glory to God in the highest*, with response as loud and as melodic from the opposite point, *and on earth peace, good will toward men!*

From the boy's lips came, in whispered declaration, "Messiah! Messiah! Messiah!"

Other than occasional scampers with hastened retreats to the inn courtyard, he had not until these moments previously braved the Bethlehem darkness. Sometimes, in troubled dreams, he ventured among these streets at night, encountering fearful happenings.

But he had settled in his mind that this was not a dream. The sky was real, the star, the singing, the taking of the chalice and the commission to "go and make known." Ah, yes, Elysmus, the son of Bal Nahor, was full awake and set upon the most important task of his young lifetime.

But then, in one terrifying moment, he forgot the star and the song as a small group of shepherds stepped into his way. The leader, burly and tall, caught him with strong grasp.

"Boy!" he exclaimed in a rasping voice.

Elysmus looked up into the man's face, distinct in the radiance of the overhead star. Skin bronzed by the sun and by sand and wind, eyes long adapted to the night, the shepherd so frightened the boy he could scarcely move his lips in a soundless effort to cry for help.

"Zuar!" a second shepherd scolded. "Each moment has a talent's worth to us. Waste no time on a mere child!"

"I tell you again," said another of the herdsmen, "it is not for sinners like us to go searching. It's not for shepherds with blood on their hands. Whatever it is you saw or heard, leave it to the priests and rabbis. Let us return to the lambs. Agreed?"

"I command you to silence, Diderus!" Zuar exclaimed. "You as well, Enosh! All of you!"

"Fools are known by both their words and their silences," Diderus replied, defying his leader's injunction.

"Zuar is our chief shepherd, Diderus," Enosh interceded gently. "We are to obey him."

"Obey him when we watch our flocks," Diderus retorted, "but not when he leads us like blind men through such benighted darkness."

Elysmus glanced back toward the inn with a moment's longing for its assuring walls. He looked up at big Zuar and wished for courage and strength to wrench himself free. Indeed, he might have made the attempt except for the singing.

Glory to God in the highest!

Louder and more beautiful than before.

On earth peace, good will toward men!

"Messiah," the boy whispered.

"What was that you said?" Zuar demanded. He all but lifted Elysmus from the ground to look down at him the more intently. "What did you just say?"

"Nothing, Sir," Elsymus whimpered.

"Nothing?" the big man scoffed. "Every word of Jehovah's making is something. There is no nothing."

"He spoke his father's name," Diderus suggested.

"Who is your father?" Zuar asked. "Per chance he could help us. Who is he?"

"My father is Bal Nahor."

"Bal Nahor? Who in seven Sabbaths is Bal Nahor? A scribe? One who reads the scrolls and knows the traditions?"

"Then he could assist us in our search!" Enosh suggested.

"Is your father a man of the synagogue?" Zuar asked.

"My father is the innkeeper," the boy answered.

"Innkeeper," the big shepherd repeated in gruff disappointment.

"I have heard about Bethlehem's innkeeper!" Diderus sang out. "He is all or more as much a thief and scoundrel as I am." He nudged Elysmus with his staff. "Out following your sire's footsteps, is it? Looking for something to pilfer?" In a tone of voice feigning camaraderie, the shepherd added, "We could teach you a trick or two. Now, for example. . . ."

"Quiet, Diderus," Zuar demanded.

Then, with a sweep of his strong hand, the big man thrust Elysmus forward with such force that, but for his nimbleness, the boy could have fallen.

He stood a moment, drawn to these men as much as fearing them.

"Shall we speak with this innkeeper?" Enosh asked.

"Of what use could he be to us?" Zuar questioned gruffly.

"Of no use," Enosh responded in quiet agreement.

The chief shepherd gestured for the others to follow him. All did so but one.

"You, Diderus," Zuar called out. "Come with us or return to the flocks."

Diderus hesitated another moment. Then he moved forward.

"I come with you," he said compliantly.

Chapter Five

The way to Arphaxad's house led through the town center, a place of quietness on usual days in little Bethlehem and of silence at nightfall. Now, however, as the innkeeper's son approached the area, clamoring sounds and raucous voices gave gentle Bethlehem the madness of Jerusalem's cacophony when sellers and buyers thronged about the Damascus gate on first day mornings.

The startled boy took hasty refuge behind an ox cart.

Before him a throng of strangers and townsfolk milled about or sat at evening fires. Women and children huddled in more distant sites . . . some with fire, some without . . . faring as best they could.

Occasional tents bordered the area, sheltering inhabitants able to afford such luxury. A cluster of men, drunken like the innkeeper, joined in boisterous dissonance to render an obscene song about a slave girl and her Pharisee master. Weary hustlers clustered among their donkeys and camels. Most slept. Some cast dice by the light of the common fire. Others chattered and shared their wine.

"Oil and meal," a Bethlehem merchant cried out. "Buy from me. My price is fair."

"Fair?" someone scowled, "Only if four times the normal price is fair."

A camel, frightful in strange surroundings, sent people scurrying as it ran about the enclosure and then out into the night.

"If that is my animal," one drunk called out, "there will be one less groomsman for the Romans to count!"

Laughter applauded the remark.

"Praises to Jehovah!" exclaimed one man scarcely able to form words. "Nowhere in all Judea excels David's country for the fruit of the vine."

"We journeyed to Bethlehem from Gadara," said another. "In the best of years, our grapes are like the tip of your smallest finger and our wines savor the tongue scarce more than does water."

"I dwell in the lowness of Idumea," said a third, "where wine reaches us only by caravan."

"Why lament inferior wines," someone called out, "when we have Judah's best in ample store? I say we drink to Caesar Augustus whose decree brings us to this joyful gathering."

A cheer approved the statement. Lifted wineskins brought the acclaimed nectar to momentarily silenced lips.

"Stop! Stop!" a voice broke the silence. "Drink not to the gods of Rome. Drink to our silent Jehovah. There has not been a prophet in four hundred years, much less the Promised One."

Wine skins were lowered.

In the brief silence, Elysmus looked about the darkness. Except for warming fires, town center lay in the clutches of the night. Looking up, however, he beheld the star in all its brightness. Beyond the crowded area, he saw the dim outline of the synagogue. Yet, he could not summon courage to continue toward the home of his teacher.

"Piety?" the first man said, as though sobering. "The Romans executed my eldest son for singing David's song about the waters of Meribah. 'Sing only in the synagogue and during the Sabbath,' they told him. On a cross they nailed him, as innocent as the day of his mother's sorrow. Where is Jehovah's justice now with my son rotting in his grave?"

No one responded.

"You speak like a Samaritan," a voice carried out of the darkness. "Gehenna for those who blaspheme."

"Blasphemy? We invoke reality, not blasphemy. For the span of a man's lifetime, Egypt held our people captive. Babylonia bent their backs in servitude. Assyria . . . what was it, three jubilees? Four? Always, in those dark times, prophets led the way. But we? Under the curse of Malachi, now and ever more!"

"Four hundred years and no prophet!"

"We will suffer under Rome forever!"

"I heard a centurion and his armored man talking," one of the Bethlehem merchants said. Elysmus recognized his voice and was comforted. "They gave the reason for the census."

"Reason?" another scoffed. "A show of Rome's authority is the only reason."

"That to be sure," the merchant agreed, "but there is yet another cause. The census is like the time the new king in Egypt feared the growing population of the Israelites. Surely you remember that story from an early portion from Exodus"

"How do you say that?" someone asked.

"By what I heard of this centurion," was the reply. "A census in Rome distressed the Emperor to the quick. The counting revealed how men agree to marriage and fatherhood. Census taking among citizens in other parts of the empire manifested similarity. Know it to be sure, once mighty Rome is in decay."

"Caesar Augustus need not fret about prolific Hebrews," a man from Nazareth exclaimed. "He will be pleased with me. In the words of our kinsman, *"Blessed is the man whose quiver is full."* Take my example. Seven sons and. . . ." he paused. Lifting the wineskin he drank heavily. "In my present state," he quipped, "I cannot remember how many daughters."

Attention was drawn to a troubadour who kept rhythm with a timbrel as he intoned a portion of a Psalm. *"The Lord says to my Lord: sit at my right hand until I make your enemies a footstool."*

"Enough, minstrel." A man from Jericho, his wits awash in alcohol, stumbled toward the singer. "Intone no more. A centurion sleeps within earshot."

The intruder drank deeply from his wineskin. Then, his warning having been but a ruse to draw attention to himself, he faltered to and fro as, pretending himself a prophet, he expounded to those who would listen.

"Messiah comes at next Passover!"

"Verily! Verily!" a man of equal intoxication affirmed.

"We shall see the blood of Herod's swordsmen flowing in our streets."

"Verily! Verily!" exclaimed others.

"The stink of Roman flesh will fertilize Hebrew fields. Sword and armor will rust and decay. Ours shall be the trade routes . . . the skins of Ethiopia . . . the bangles of Phoenicia . . . the jewels of Egypt. Every Hebrew shall have his own palace. The fairest maidens of the forum shall be ours to summon and enjoy."

Approving laughter came from listeners.

As the laughter lingered, a pair of Roman soldiers brushed past Elysmus, startling him. They walked briskly into the hub of activity and, without speaking, took the self-styled forcteller into custody. Too intoxicated to assess what was happening, the man submitted as though his arrest was some ceremony of honor.

"Hail, Caesar!" he called out.

"Hail fruit of the vine!" someone contradicted.

But there was no laughter. The act of Roman authority brought the most intoxicated into fearful respect. Taking this as his opportunity and summoning all the courage his pounding heart could muster, Elysmus poised his trembling body for a dash forward.

Dare he go?

Glory to God in the highest!

The song caused him to look upward, up to the star of wonder.

"Go and make known!" It was as though the angel had spoken a second time.

Angel?

If an angel commanded, angels would protect!

"O Jehovah," he whispered.

Chapter Six

Elysmus gained confidence as he watched men in the town center move about like harmless shadows. The display of Rome's dominion had smitten them with temporary sobriety. Ominous silence became as pervading as the previous tumult. Surely he could now go safely to the house of his teacher. Yet, for all his resolve, fear held the boy inert. When he did move, it was to look back toward the inn.

"*In the day when I cried out,*" he remembered from David's writings, "*you answered me and made me bold with strength in my soul.*"

"Make me bold, O great Jehovah," he whispered.

He had but finished the prayer when the night's prior activity slowly resumed. Mumbling voices. Lifted wineskins. Then a drunken stranger began to dance. Twisting and turning in bacchanalian orgy, he put off all but the scantest of his clothes. The crowd cheered approval.

Elysmus had never seen such wickedness. How angry his mother would be if she knew he permitted his eyes to behold these evil doings.

Looking again toward town center, he saw the performer pretend to be a woman of lust and passion. Others joined the portrayal. Some of the men accosted the performer. A few also pretended to be women, imitating the near-naked reveler, simulating his obscene gestures, adding their discordant voices to his in lascivious serenade.

Surely Elysmus had no choice but return to the inn.

Also, as he lingered now, fearful of crossing the town center, he experienced his first uncertainty as to whether it would be, in fact, a foolish act to summon his teacher. Arphaxad himself, in spite of his partial blindness, had surely seen the star and heard the angels and was even now walking about Bethlehem on a proclaiming mission of his own. Like Jeremiah, perhaps, he was weeping and shouting, declaring the holy event.

No, Elysmus should return to the inn!

Yet, in that moment, clearly as in an echo, he heard again the angel's command, "Go and make known!"

The angel had spoken to him, to Elysmus, to a boy, one of many children who ran and played in Bethlehem's streets.

He took what was meant to be a final glance at town center, at the vileness and the clamor and the confusion. When he turned away, a burst of light came downward with such vigor it was like lightning that struck and sustained its intensity. Elysmus fell to the ground. With the overhead brilliance came also increased singing, a vast choir of celestial voices.

"Glory to God in the highest, and on earth peace, good will toward men!"

Before him the village center and its cavorting throng lay in darkness relieved only by the warming fires while he himself stood in a circle of light. From wise King Solomon,

Elysmus remembered the words from his proverbs, *"He holds victory in store for the upright. He is a shield to those whose walk is blameless."* He also recalled from the song of David, *"You will not fear the terror of night."*

Forgetting his uncertainty, and with the boldness of the boy David in his advance toward Goliath, Elysmus sprinted forward. *"In Your presence is fullness of joy,"* he said, fortifying his courage with words from another of David's Psalms.

Into the carousing throng he ran. Some in their drunkenness did not see him. Others watched with startled curiosity. No one hindered his progress. Between tethered camels he scampered, alongside a Bethlehem merchant smoothing and folding silks for next day selling. So easy was the passage, boyhood delight became more dominant than fear.

But then, like the forward strike of a desert viper, a man's arm encircled Elysmus. The boy was tossed like a ball into the air. As he descended, again held in the firm grip of his captor, he looked into the face of a man similar in size and appearance to Zuar, the shepherd.

"Ho, little hellion," the man roared, his words festooned by raw laughter. "What is it Ben Ahmed of Zebulon finds in the darkness of David's village? Run you to or run you from? Be you an orphan? A child of the night? Some madam's solicitor?"

Elysmus kicked and squirmed but found himself as firmly as though bound by strong fetters. His eyes turned heavenward in search of hope just as a cloud moved across the star, dimming its light, numbing his spirits.

"Ho, ye!" the man cried. He lifted the boy and held him high for all to see. A company of strangers gathered quickly.

"A slave boy we have here," Ben Ahmed intoned. "How

much is the first bid?

"Half a denarius!" someone jested.

"Robbery," Ben Ahmed reprimanded. "I would myself wager a pouch of silverling."

A man came running from the outer shadows. "My jubilee amulet!" he screamed. "Someone stole it."

"Perhaps this boy of the night is a thief," Ben Ahmed shouted, as much in amusement as in accusation.

The big man turned Elysmus upright, holding him by one leg and shaking him as one would do to empty the contents of a bagskin. He stood the boy onto his feet, continuing the firm grasp, and searched every nook of his garments.

"No amulet," Ben Ahmed announced.

Another man appeared beside the boy's accuser. He held a consumed wineskin. "See here, you fool!" He removed an object from the neck of the container and offered it to the man. "You took off the jewel to lessen the sin of your drunkenness."

The man took the item. He lifted it into the flicker of Ben Ahmed's night fire. "You are the fool," he retorted. "You are drunker than I am." He held up the supposed jewel for the other man's closer inspection. "This came loose from my camel's bridle."

The man from the shadows looked at Elysmus for a moment and then changed his manner.

"Amulet or camel's haltering," he mumbled, "what does it matter?"

He moved close to Elysmus who thereby saw dimly the pallor of the stranger's cheeks and caught fully the smell of his fetid breath.

"Let me relieve you of this youngling from the flock," the man said, looking up at Ben Ahmed. As he turned his attention to Elysmus, he whispered loudly, "Have you yet shared your passion with animals? What know you of the pleasures of Sodom?"

Ben Ahmed overheard. His swift and mighty kick to the groin sent the man writhing to the ground. Ben Ahmed glanced but a moment at the one he had put down. He then turned to Elysmus and said, "Ben Ahmed of Zebulon will keep you for himself. What a fine serving boy you could be. Not a slave, mind you. A servant paid a wage."

A nearby camel snorted for attention.

"Ho, now," Ben Ahmed exclaimed happily. "Bring water to my camels as your first performance in my employment."

A woman came out of the shadows.

"You gave me your amulet as payment for my services," the woman said to the man who writhed in agony upon the ground. She tossed the ornament. "Take it, lest I bear a curse for having received a sacred item as adulterous defrayment."

By fire light, Elysmus recognized the woman as Megira, the night woman. He looked upon her with the same misgivings he held toward the shepherds.

"It is the innkeeper's son," Megira said. "I have not seen his father since the Feast of Harvest." Of Elysmus, she asked, "What brings you here at an hour when no children are about?"

Even as she spoke, the overhead cloud reopened, revealing the star.

"Look!" Elysmus shouted.

"Glory to God in the highest!"

"The singing!" Elysmus added. "Hear the singing! See Messiah's star!"

"Messiah?" asked Megira in a startled voice. "The

Promised One?"

"Messiah is born this night!"

"In Bethlehem?"

"In my father's stable!"

"The boy is a prophet," a drunken visitor exclaimed.

"Messiah," from another, "birthed in sheep manure?"

Bleating and laughing, a group of men bantered among themselves.

"Did you hear, gentle lambs? Did you hear?"

"Yes, you old goat."

"Did you hear the donkeys?"

"Yes, you camel."

Laughter rose and fell across Bethlehem's town center as intoxicated men discontinued their sensual simulations and began scantering about like animals. They jostled each other. Some fell to the earth and caused others to stumble. They bleated and brayed and crowed. A group to one side had been contesting the separate values of their provinces and now found excuse for combat.

"The boy is a devil!" Ben Ahmed of Zebulon gasped. "See what his blasphemy has done!" He released Elysmus.

"What are you telling us?" Megira asked the innkeeper's son. Her voice was tender like a mother's, eager like a child's.

Elysmus did not respond. For he thought he saw the star cast a flicker of light upon Megira's face. He looked up at the man from Zebulon who stood in darkness.

"I must go to the house of Arphaxad, my teacher," Elysmus said. "I will tell him Messiah has come."

"The boy is not mad," a man nearby overheard Elysmus and called out, "He proclaims the truth. Let us all drink to it.

Messiah has come to make us free men, free and rich."

"My house shall be of marble," exclaimed a second man.

"With an outhouse of alabaster," another added.

More was spoken but uproars of laughter obscured the voices.

"I wish to go with you," the woman said to Elysmus. "On second thought," she mumbled, "would Arphaxad, the holy one, permit the appearance of Megira, the sinful one?"

She placed her hand upon the boy's shoulder, as his mother had so often done, and the two walked together into the shadows.

"Woman?" a man cried angrily. "You promised your services as soon as I emptied my wineskin. I'm too drunk to eat but sober enough. . . ." The mention of food gave the man momentary nausea.

Megira hesitated, holding firmly to the boy's shoulder. Elysmus saw another quick cast of star light fall upon her face.

"Where are you, woman?" the man continued. "I could fancy beating you as much as ravishing you."

Megira slowly turned away from Elysmus.

"Go to your teacher," she said. "Anyone so holy would curse the sight of such as I."

She proceeded back toward the night fires.

CHAPTER SEVEN

Overhead clouds withdrew allowing full presence to the Advent Star. Elysmus moderated his progress to better witness the spectacle. As he walked, the din of town center carousing disrupted his enthrallment. Only for a moment, however, for angelic encore resounded from the skies to engulf the whole of Bethlehem in wondrous point and counterpoint.

"Glory to God in the highest. . . ."

"Messiah!" Elysmus exclaimed as he proceeded bounding into leaps half again his normal stride.

Star glow lighted the pathway, falling upon the rejoicing boy like sunshine, warming his excited being from flesh to marrow. The music's crescendo reduced his shouting to the clarity of a whisper. Halting his progress a second time, he looked out at the streets and dwellings. Most Bethlehem houses were of humble construction, erected out of limestone fragments held in place by thick applications of clay. An occasional residence, belonging to some well-positioned family, was built of hewn stone mortared with gypsum brought up from the Salt Sea.

Loud coughing emerged from one house, a child's drowsy lament from another. Mostly, however, the residences stood dark and silent. At times, the boy's footfalls became so loud he would have removed his sandals but for the night air's crispness. Lest he cause disturbance, he proceeded with increasing caution, coming to a rise in the town's elevation from which he could look past the populated area to the far-extending shepherd's fields, star-lit, as was he, by Messiah's proclaiming sky. He did not initially take note that, while Bethlehem lay in darkness, those fields radiated with light. Instead, he thought of the many times he played in those fields, times when he set aside his fantasies of David and pretended to be the prophet Micah. Romping from terrace to terrace, he would quote the Messiah prophecy as though in announcement to the whole of Judea.

"Bethlehem Eprhatah, though you are small among the clans of Judah. . . ."

He frequently repeated the words. His youthful pulse quickened by rapture and realization. So exalted were the boy's thoughts on some of those occasions, he would quote his own composition.

"The sky is Thine, the sun and the moon. . . ."

The sky?

Elysmus abruptly discontinued his jubilation for, in this moment, as he looked out toward the horizon, it now occurred to him that, even as it also encircled him, the glow of the glorious star touched hill and vale with silvered essence.

Star light!

Singing!

How could anyone remain asleep? Why did not the whole of Bethlehem arise to herald this majesty?

A new thought came to Elysmus.

What of Arphaxad?

Did he sleep?

How could such a pious person slumber, he who so eloquently spoke of the Promised One, the tip of whose tongue . . . like the scrolls themselves . . . held in store the splendid language of prophetic declarations?

How dare he disturb such a man? The boy's mother likened Arphaxad to Elijah! Even now his teacher was surely standing on the portico to his dwelling, his aged ears attuned to the heavenly carol, his feeble eyes intent upon the announcing star.

"But you, Bethlehem Ephratah. . . ."

It was as though Elysmus could hear his teacher's voice blending in harmony with the angel choir. Or perhaps . . . it was a startling thought . . . Arphaxad had also taken to the streets. On ahead, if he dared continue, Elysmus and the teacher would meet.

Would Arphaxad embrace him?

Or, in anger, would he demand his return to the inn?

In that moment, Elysmus seemed once again to hear the angel's command, "Go and make known!"

Surely the same angel had similarly commissioned Arphaxad. Or could it be that, like the boy Samuel, the boy Elysmus had been chosen to bear first tidings of this glorious time? What a wonder it would be giving the news to his teacher, or, as likely, see him at his doorway looking up at the sky and listening to the angels. Watching Arphaxad during such moments would be akin to having seen Micah and Isaiah!

As well as Samuel and David!

So, with measured steps, Elysmus continued onward.

He could not restrain his enthusiasm for the angel song transitioned into harmony so melodic the boy felt himself a part of the music.

How could anyone remain silent?

"Messiah! Messiah!" he announced with fullest breath. "He is born this night in Bethlehem! As the prophet wrote: *Bethlehem Ephratah, though you are small among the clans of Judah. . . .*"

Elysmus would have continued shouting but in that moment was struck by an object hurtling out of the darkness and hitting him with such force he fell to the cobbled surface of the street.

"Maniac!" a voice called out from the nearest house. "Who loosed your chains?"

Elysmus stood. He had been hit at shoulder tip and moved his arm to test the injury.

"What is it?" a man stepped forward. "A boy?" His voice became more consoling. "Walking asleep? This night's dream frightens you?"

He came to Elysmus and shook him vigorously.

"Wake up, boy! Wake up!"

"I am awake, sir." Elysmus managed to say. He winced from the pain where he had been struck by the thrown object.

"Awake, you say?" the man asked. "Then why this foolish roaming about Bethlehem to disturb the sleep of your townsmen? Or were you hired by one of the visitors to plague us with their displeasures of Caesar's latest decree? Taking a census is more Roman lunacy, as everyone knows, of no purpose whatever to the people of Judea. But we all languish equally."

The disgruntled sleeper prattled on in a fluent tirade

about the injustices of Roman servitude, as though he had audience of many and not merely one boy who understood little of what he heard.

"My father is Bal Nahor," Elysmus managed to say when the spurious orator paused for a moment's breath.

"And, further, I would add. . . ."

The man paused abruptly. He grasped Elysmus by the chin and turned his face upward. "Bal Nahor, did you say?"

"I did, sir."

With a flaunting thrust, the man sent Elysmus sprawling a second time. He came and stood over him, a hulking and fearsome silhouette made the more ominous with no glint of the miraculous light illuminating his face or person.

"I have it now!" the infuriated townsman thundered. "You are a thief in the same manner as your deceitful forbear. He double-charged my wife and me when we used his inn's squalid facilities for our daughter's wedding. Your father is a deceiver, sired in the bloodline of Beliel!"

Elysmus attempted to rise but was put down by a swift kick.

"Please, sir," the boy pleaded.

"A thief! A thief!" The man cupped his hands to his mouth. "Guards! Soldiers! Hail Caesar!"

They stood a moment, waiting, looking about.

"Voice a word's complaint about the Empire, and a squad of Roman soldiers drags a man to Golgatha," he grumbled. "Need them and they are nowhere."

The man put his foot to the boy's throat, lightly choking him. The fate of Elysmus might have been sorry, indeed, had not a subsequent object come pelting out of the darkness. This one struck the anger-crazed man with such force he fell gasping alongside his terrified prey.

"How dare you disturb the night?" a voice cried out. Other protests followed as a hand's measure of men, neighbors in the vicinity gathered around the man and the boy.

Elysmus ventured cautiously to his feet. His oppressor slowly stood as well. Whereupon the neighbors began loudly shouting, first at the one whose harangue had disturbed them, then among themselves. The darkness enhanced utterances some would never dare to speak in daylight, neighbor-versus-neighbor complaints and criticisms long subdued by propriety.

"The singing, honorable, sirs!" Elysmus proclaimed with courage beyond his years.

"What singing?" came a chorused outcry.

"It is the angels, for Messiah is born this night . . . ."

"Born where?" a man interrupted.

"In Bethlehem."

"Where in Bethlehem?" Looking about, the man gestured toward the surrounding town, motionless in the night's darkness. "Where, I say?"

"At the inn."

"Bal Nahor's inn? Messiah born in such a destitute habitat? If I had swine in need of shelter, I would bed them outdoors before driving them into that benighted place!"

"Not the inn," Elysmus said cautiously, "the stable. Messiah is born in my father's stable."

Banter and accusations were laid aside as, in the manner of men at town center, the neighbors made sport of the boy's words.

Elysmus took the opportunity to slip away unnoticed. He

walked several paces, then glanced back to see the men of the neighborhood closed in by darkness. Only continued chattering gave evidence of their presence.

Overhead, the star shined with sustaining brightness and the song of the angels continued in countless varieties of rendition and exaltation.

CHAPTER EIGHT

For all his awe and awareness, his abounding enthusiasm and reinforced courage, Elysmus continued passage toward the home of his teacher with cautious steps. He kept his ears attuned to the sound of approaching footsteps and his eyes alert for the sight of Arphaxad, himself seeking the Messiah.

The boy's mind was awhirl with questions and concerns beyond the usual thinking of anyone so young.

Even though Arphaxad frequently complimented him for his prowess in synagogue studies, Elysmus could not settle his mind on the right of a boy to call upon such a revered person without being summoned to do so. Even if he might so venture by daylight, could it be inappropriate, perhaps insulting, to come unannounced in the darkness?

Yet, he knew with surest certainty his great teacher's yearning for the promises to be fulfilled.

The innkeeper's son also thought of days at the synagogue when, his eyes more weakened than other days, Arphaxad called upon his students to read the sacred scrolls. So the great man might know of Messiah's birth but dared not venture into

Bethlehem's darkness.

Lingering in the boy's ears, as though the words had been just spoken, was the angel's command to "go and make known." He had tried at town center and had broken the silence in proclamation among the dwellings only to be rebuked. Yet, he must not despair because first to his mind, when the angel had spoken, was to summon his teacher.

Within the fortnight Arphaxad had read from the scrolls of Moses, *"The Lord your God will raise up for you a prophet like me from your midst, from your brethren. Him you shall hear."*

A tear had moistened the eye of the teacher as he lowered the scroll to look out at his students and said: "In those ancient days, Moses foresaw the coming Messiah. Scant wonder the great patriarch's face glowed with heaven's light. One can wonder who would have dared enter into the lawgiver's presence at that time. Perhaps not even members of his own family."

Arphaxad was a man like Moses. Many times, when the esteemed teacher read the scrolls and spoke of their meaning, Elysmus imagined himself as a shepherd listening to Elijah, the boy's favorite among the ancients. As often, the son of the innkeeper pretended to be the boy Samuel hearing from the lips of Eli words of preparation for holy service.

But while assuming Arphaxad surely knew of this night's glory, lingering in the boy's heart were the words of the angel. It was beyond his supposing that Jehovah had chosen him to bear the tidings, yet, remembering the child Samuel, he wondered if, indeed, such might be the circumstance.

Elysmus had seen adults brought to judgment for unintentional neglect of one of the lesser Levitical laws. Was there sustained in the scrolls some decree condemning children who engaged in conduct disrespectful to men skilled in the laws of Moses and the prophets?

"Glory to God in highest. . . ."

The angel song continued in beauteous melody filling the boy's heart with expanding delight. How dare a child such as he experience so great joy? Would the elders rebuke him if they knew, his parents be brought to shame and dishonor?

Even as those thoughts came to him, Elysmus remembered.

Arphaxad spoke of the ecstasy coming upon the prophets when they, apart from all the others, experienced divine predictions and wonders. Elysmus retained doubts of a mere boy standing properly in the presence of one who clearly saw this night's wonder as the culmination of centuries-long promise and expectancy. Would such a boy have dared to look upon Micah when he wrote the ancient prophecy? Or Isaiah when he foretold the virgin and her son?

Yet, what of the angel's command?

And what of his abounding joy?

In the full of his heart, Elysmus believed this to be the night of Micah's prophecy.

"Perhaps I alone have seen the light of the star." The boy tried to assure himself. "To my ears only has come the singing." As Jehovah chose the boy Samuel, could he not choose the boy, Elysmus, to hear the first word of the Promised One's coming?

Arphaxad, like Eli in the temple, may have thus far been denied.

"Glory to God in the highest. . . ."

"Messiah's song!" the boy cried.

Elysmus looked up, the light so intense he held his hand

to his eyes.

"Messiah's Star!"

He proceeded, whispering as he walked, "*You, Bethlehem Ephratah, though you are small among the clans of Judah, out of you will come for me one who will be ruler over Israel.*"

Then, suddenly, a snarling guard dog emerged out of the darkness leaping toward Elysmus in full attack. The boy's first thought was that this was a demon serving Jehovah as an agent of judgment.

Elysmus fell to his knees.

The dog halted progress within reach of the terrified boy. The animal stood there, teeth barred, poised as though for further attack, yet unmoving.

"O great Jehovah!" Elysmus whispered.

Scarcely knowing that he did it, the innkeeper's son held out the back of his hand.

The dog did not bite. It licked the boy's hand. In awe, Elysmus stood. The dog whimpered, then turned and reverted to the shadows from which it had come.

"O great Jehovah!" Elysmus said aloud as he turned and continued progress toward Arphaxad's residence.

CHAPTER NINE

Supposing the encounter with the guard dog a token of Jehovah's approval and guidance, Elysmus proceeded with renewed motive. In one moment the whims of boyhood came upon him, and he leaped and danced with delight. In the next instant his young mind was stretched by thoughts beyond childhood experience or insight.

The second emotion prevailed. As he came nearer to the house of Arphaxad, he walked with steps more measured than ever he had entered the synagogue for festival services or approached the city gate when the elders of Bethlehem sat in council.

As the Advent Star lighted his path with continuing brightness and the song of the angels lingered across the night, the boy increasingly wondered how it could be he alone beheld.

Yet, continually in his mind, the angel's command quieted any concerns or questions.

"Go and make known!"

Surely it was a divine command.

From the scrolls of Moses, Arphaxad had read: *"Keep the*

commands of the Lord Jehovah."

In tears, Arphaxad once spoke David's words about angels and their service as guardians and guides. *"He shall give His angels charge over you,"* the teacher sang in quavering ecstasy that day, *"to keep you in all your ways."*

"Mostly," Arphaxad explained, "angels guide us beyond our seeing." The aged and venerable teacher had then paused for lengthy interim after which, speaking loudly and in words aglow with warning as well as inspiration, he declared, "If in His goodness Jehovah permits you to look upon an angel or if you hear an angel's voice, you must be most reverent of heart and obedient of mind and body."

Why had Elysmus not recalled this counsel until now? Did angels in their ministering guide one's thoughts? Had an angel reminded him of this important learning from his studies?

"Glory to God in the highest . . . ." sang the angel chorus.

Above, like a lamp in the very hand of Jehovah, the Advent Star penetrated the night.

Then, as if spoken directly behind him, came the words: "Go and make known!"

Elysmus turned quickly.

He saw nothing.

"Mostly angels guide us beyond our seeing," Arphaxad had said.

"Go and make known!"

"If you hear with your ears an angel's voice," the respected teacher further said, "you must be most reverent of heart and obedient of mind and body."

Elysmus thought of the angel who received the chalice at the stable cave entrance, who uttered the command: "Go and make known!" Was this exalted being also a member of the sky choir, chosen from among them to provide services for the Messiah child? Was such an angel at his side now? Did a company of guardians surround him as he ventured through Bethlehem's darkness? Would such beings bless his arrival at the home of Arphaxad, using him as their messenger?

Even as the boy Samuel had been used?

And the boy David?

Thinking anew of the adventures of the boy Samuel, Elysmus whispered, "Speak, Lord, for your servant hears."

He experienced a moment abundant with joy and determination. In the wake of the emotion, however, came foreboding. If, indeed, Jehovah had chosen the lips of a boy in Bethlehem to bear the first tidings of Messiah's coming, then Arphaxad himself did not know. His deafness may have kept his sleep undisturbed. His weak sight may have shielded the starlight from his notice.

"How will I speak to him?" Elysmus said aloud, in both prayer and apprehension.

Then, to his mind distinctly, came an episode from the scrolls: *"Moses said to Jehovah, 'I am slow of speech and tongue.' Jehovah said to him, 'Go. I will help you speak and will teach your what to say.'"*

It was one emotion to sit at the feet of a great teacher in childhood wonderment and then stand alone on the streets of Bethlehem, daring to believe the words could become living experience in his own life.

"Speak, Lord, for Your servant hears!" Elysmus cried out.

In the wake of his own utterance came the words of the angel, "Go and make known!"

Weeping and laughing, running and halting, leaping, stumbling, hilarious with joy, mindful of lingering fear, the innkeeper's son continued his mission.

CHAPTER TEN

A boy named Elysmus, as one having become a man years before his time, proceeded with both careful and confident step across the length of Bethlehem's streets to a small rise where he paused to look upon the house of his teacher.

Starlight encompassed the innkeeper's son like a cloak of choicest linen, elegance surpassing the blues and purples and scarlets worn by the high priest at temple services, more protective than a centurion's armor, beyond boyhood's imagined fantasies, a phenomenon as real to Elysmus as it was astounding. Similarly, the Advent Anthem became wondrously intimate, as though crafted within him, his flesh and marrow reverberating with melody and joy.

"Blessed are the people who know the joyful sound," he remembered synagogue lessons from Psalms. *"They walk, O Jehovah, in the light of your presence!"*

The thought reverted his attention to the scene before him, to his beloved teacher but also to the first realization that the heralding Star withheld its light from the stone hewn residence. Silent as death it stood, its windows drawn and dark.

"Messiah!" he gasped. "My teacher does not know!"

Elysmus quickly traversed the short distance remaining.

"Messiah! Messiah!" he cried as he scampered onto the portico of Arphaxad's house. "O my teacher! Come and see!"

He grasped the bronze knocker and clacked it forcefully against the bronze facing of the elaborately garnished door.

"Messiah has come, my teacher!" he shouted. Even in the hour's excitement, he attempted to be careful in the choice of words. "Messiah! The Promised One of whom you teach us!"

"Glory to God in the highest!"

A cloak of darkness fell now upon the portico obliterating the fine jurassic limestone brought from Lebanon for the building's construction. The darkness evoked a silence so dense it barricaded the structure against the sights and sounds of the night. Elysmus looked up to the Advent Star shining but with a thickening cloud moving across it causing intermittent bursts of light. The song became muffled, intensity lessened.

The boy felt his courage wane.

But he continued knocking.

Perhaps his teacher *had* heard the angels. Perhaps his teacher *had* seen the star. In a moment of imagining, Elysmus envisioned the venerable teacher standing at this moment in the stable holding the newborn Messiah in his arms, the angel by his side.

So, had the son of the innkeeper done wrong in coming to Arphaxad's residence?

Did his wrong explain the silence and darkness?

Was the angel's command to "go and make known" intended only for those revelers at town center? Having announced the news to them, ought he to have gone back to the inn?

"Have I a visitor at this hour?" Arphaxad was questioning in a drowsy and quavering voice.

A soft creaking occurred as faltering hands slipped back the hardwood beriah, allowing the door to open. Arphaxad, dressed in his night clothes, appeared inquiringly. He held a dimly-flamed oil light and moved it forward and downward to determine the identity of his visitor.

"Who is it?" he asked. "My eyes fail me in this light."

"I am Elysmus."

"Elysmus! My favorite among the students!" There was both praise and apprehension in the halting voice. "Are you troubled? Do you bear bad tidings?"

The boy moved his tongue about in his mouth searching for a response. Then, clearly once more, the angel chorus continued the pronouncement.

"Glory to God in the highest. . . ."

Starlight touched the roof's edge of the portico coming down once more upon Elysmus. He studied the old man's countenance for a hint of recognition.

". . . on earth peace, good will to men."

"It is Messiah's singing," the boy ventured cautiously.

"Singing, Elysmus?" the old teacher asked gruffly. "What singing?"

"And the Sta. . . ."

But as Elysmus looked out upon the darkness, cloud-cover moved rapidly and completely across the sky. With equal abruptness, the angels' song went silent. A slash of lightning preceded loud thunder and a heavy down flow of rain.

"Star?" Arphaxad asked. "Singing?"

Elysmus stood in stunned silence.

"You are dreaming!" Arphaxad insisted. It was as though he sought to be compassionate but could not restrain the sting of reproof in his voice.

Elysmus, weeping, fell to his knees, and in panic embraced the legs of the old man.

"You came here in your sleep," Arphaxad said, more kindly now. "You have been dreaming."

"O my teacher," Elysmus managed above his sobbing, "I am fully awake."

"Quiet, Elysmus," the old man scolded lightly. "Do not intrude upon the speaking of your teacher."

Arphaxad lifted Elysmus to his feet and moved him toward the doorway.

"Come inside. I have fresh milk." He remained in the doorway, looking out at the pelting rain. "I will fix you a place to rest. You cannot return to the inn in this weather."

"I have not been dreaming!" Elysmus insisted. "My words are true! Messiah has come! He is born this night in Bethlehem!"

During all his years at the synagogue, in times when Arphaxad would express displeasure, Elysmus had never seen such an expression come upon the old man's face. His countenance became like granite, his eyes like spear points, and he fashioned his lips in the snarl of an angered jackal.

"Messiah?" the old man scoffed. "You blaspheme! You mock the name of Jehovah."

"I speak the truth!"

Arphaxad struck Elysmus across the mouth.

"Believe my words!" Elysmus pleaded. "Messiah has come. An angel sent me to tell you. It is true! True!"

For a long interim, the teacher and the student looked intently at each other. Like hoarfrost in a morning's warmth, the anger diminished on the old man's face. He formed his lips to speak, but his speech faltered.

"O Great Jehovah," the boy prayed silently. No other words than these formed in his confused mind.

"You are an honest boy," Arphaxad began. "Perhaps you are like the boy Samuel. . . ."

The old man struggled to speak.

"O Great Jehovah," Elysmus repeated in soundless prayer.

"My heart cries out to believe," Arphaxad said at last. He gestured out across the town. "Bethlehem is silent. The ears of Arphaxad are waxen, but they would have heard the trumpets of heaven, the pronouncements of seraphs and angels."

"A man and woman came from Nazareth," Elysmus began. "They asked for room at the inn, but my father could give them none."

"What, I pray, has this to do with Messiah?"

"The woman. . . ."

Arphaxad strengthened his grip upon the boy's cloak.

"She was with child. She rode upon a donkey. She. . . ."

"You say she has birthed the Messiah?" Arphaxad scoffed.

"Yes, my teacher," Elysmus replied, "in my father's stable."

"Blasphemy!" the old man thundered. "Mock not the sacred name, Messiah! Since creation, the first word Jehovah designed for mortal utterance. When Messiah comes, He will appear as King of Kings and Lord of Lords!"

Arphaxad grew suddenly silent. As though pacing back and forth at the synagogue while expounding some teaching to his students, he mused, "I have wondered if He will sweep out of the skies in Elijah's chariot, and if Jehovah might instantaneously prepare for him a palace in the fields adjoining blessed Bethlehem. In the arms of a virgin mother, as the scrolls tell us, but with the mind and mien of a greater than Solomon."

Silent again, Arphaxad went to the doorway and looked out at the storm. A blinding flash of lightning lit him full figure, then left him again in darkness. His quavering voice became gentle as if in prayer.

"King of Kings and Lord of Lords. Messiah. True Messiah. May I live to see His coming. O Jehovah, hear the cry of your unworthy servant!"

Elysmus stood in stunned silence. He felt constrained to speak further but found no words with which to do so.

"I pray you forgive me for my anger," Arphaxad said. He placed his hands gently upon his student's shoulders. "You have had a beautiful dream. Praise the Lord Jehovah for it. At such young age, you, too, look for Messiah's coming."

Arphaxad turned and without speaking further hobbled toward his sleeping place.

"Go and make known," the boy remembered painfully.

"Messiah," he whispered, wishing to shout but unable to summon the courage or vigor.

Lightning once again lit the night.

Thunder followed.

And then the rain ceased. Elysmus hurried to the edge of the patio just as clouds once again separated and the Advent Star appeared.

The boy came quickly to Arphaxad, and led the old man to the patio's fringe.

"The star! The Star!" Elysmus cried out, pointing.

"Glory to God in the highest!"

"And the singing! The singing, O great Arphaxad!"

"What star? What singing?"

He looked up into his teacher's face and saw with horror that the old man's countenance was in darkness. Without speaking, Arphaxad turned toward his doorway. Elysmus made his way out into the night.

CHAPTER ELEVEN

As the innkeeper's son stumbled away from the home of Arphaxad, clouds once more enshrouded the sky. Drenching rain altered Bethlehem's cobbled streets into rivulets. Lightning emblazoned the heavens in thrusts as bright at times as the Advent Star had been. Thunder reverberated across town and fields like a colossus Moses crying out from distant Sinai in a lament so loudly proclaimed the whole of Judea could hear.

"I have sinned!" the boy shouted.

Bewildered.

Guilt-smitten.

He trudged on aimlessly, fearful lest the angels, whose song he no longer heard, would turn upon him in divine judgment and, their glad melody exchanged for a judicial dirge, cast him into Gehenna's depths.

"O great Jehovah!" he wailed in anguished penitence. *"Keep my soul and deliver me,"* he remembered from the scrolls of David and spoke them. *"Let me not be ashamed, for I put my trust in You."*

Aimlessly he plodded, stumbling upon the slick pavement,

his garments soaked, his body quaking from chill as penetrating as had been the intimacy of star glow and angel voices.

Again, he recalled, *"My spirit grows faint within me; my heart is dismayed."* Why had Arphaxad taught his students such sayings? Was it because, like those men at town center, the great teacher also despaired of Messiah's unending delay?

He looked up at the sky, sullen and without illumination except for lightning streaks. Soundless, as well, but for the crashing thunder. Yet, in his heart, Elysmus was sure he had seen the Star, sure he had heard the Singing.

And now, now in this moment, once again came to his mind . . . as clearly as if spoken . . . the words of his commission.

"Go and make known!"

Make known?

To whom?

Had he not been so confused, he would have avoided town center. Instead, he came directly into the open space where he had experienced so much prior anxiety. The area stood empty. Warming fires were quenched. People who could supply the fee crowded into shops or fabricated whatever shelter they could muster. Camels and donkeys stood restlessly preferring not to recline upon the water-slogged mud and slush.

"Fine night for the boy to find his Messiah," Elysmus heard one man say. Pausing long enough for a draught of wine, he added, "Innkeeper's son, didn't the lady of the night tell us?"

"I would like to meet that innkeeper alone on one of these dark streets," someone said. "I sent word with a caravan from Nazareth, when the census was first proclaimed. But when we arrived past sunfall this night, the gluttonous fool said he had no record of it."

"A mite in the hand is worth more to that man than a shekel on the horizon," someone commented. "He would deny lodging to the Messiah Himself unless the price was right."

From his crouched hiding, Elysmus once again heard the words: "Go and make known."

"To those men in town center?" he asked quietly. "Those who scoff the name of the Promised One?"

"Go and make known."

"Yes, O great Jehovah!" Elysmus whispered.

But where?

And to whom?

I am Your servant, he remembered from synagogue study. *Give me understanding.*

"I believe in Messiah's coming as much as the next person," Elysmus heard someone saying, "but if He waited four hundred years, why might he not wait four thousand?"

"Messiah?" a voice cried out.

And in that moment, the rain ceased falling. There was no more lightning, no more thunder.

"Did we hear someone speak of Messiah?" the voice continued.

The voice was unmistakably the voice of Zuar, the shepherd.

As Elysmus watched, Zuar and his small group appeared in vague silhouette a short distance away.

"We have seen His Star," Zuar said.

"We have heard the Singing Angels," affirmed the voice of Enosh.

"Somebody else gone mad!" Elysmus recognized the voice of Ben Ahmed of Zebulun.

"Can you help us?" Zuar asked.

"Go back to your flocks, shepherd." Ben Ahmed cursed and added, "Keep your thieving hands out of our purses."

Suddenly, the fissure in the clouds appeared once more. The Advent Star could be seen in full glory.

"The Star!" Zuar exclaimed, pointing.

"See it! See it!" added Enosh, joined by two other herdsmen.

"What star?" Ben Ahmed demanded. "Be thankful the rain has stopped."

Again, more clearly than ever previously, came to Elysmus the command, "Go and make known."

He hesitated one more moment, hesitated in wonder as he saw that the light of the Star fell with full illumination upon Zuar and three of his shepherds.

"I can help you!" Elysmus called out as he leaped to his feet and ran forward.

Ben Ahmed took possession of Elysmus as he had previously done.

"Look!" Enosh exulted. "This is the boy we met before. As I told you then, the Star lights his face as it does our own!"

"Madness," Ben Ahmed scoffed.

"Truthfully you speak," said Diderus. "Like madmen, we have been searching the streets of Bethlehem. . . . "

"But search no more," Elysmus interrupted, content for the moment in the arms of his captor. "Messiah is born this night."

"Can you take us to him?" Zuar questioned.

"I can," Elysmus replied.

"Truly madness," Diderus muttered.

"There seems to be one man of wits among you," said the

visitor from Zebulon. He beckoned to a servant. "Hand me the skin of wine, so I may celebrate sanity with this fellow."

Zuar reached and drew Elysmus away from Ben Ahmed's grasp. The big man gave no resistance but, instead, reached for the wine skin handed to him. This he offered to Diderus who drank from it heavily.

"Lead us," Zuar said to the innkeeper's son.

CHAPTER TWELVE

Through the remaining streets of silent Bethlehem, Elysmus and Zuar, Enosh, and two other shepherds hurried toward the inn. The Advent Star illumined their way but withheld its radiance elsewhere. An assuring calm had come to Elysmus, freeing him of apprehension for these ill-reputed men. In their first meeting, Zuar loomed over him like half-a-Goliath. Now the chief of the shepherds had a softness in his eyes and a smile upon his lips.

The Advent Star served a primary role in the boy's quietude, casting as fully upon the shepherds as onto him. Even the surrounding darkness gave added intensity to the heavenly light.

"*You, Bethlehem,*" Zuar quoted quietly, "*though you are little among the thousands of Judah . . .*"

"You know the writings!" Elysmus interrupted.

Zuar touched the boy with his staff, gently in the way he would have nudged a lamb while herding.

The chief of the shepherds continued. Elysmus joined him in unison. "*Yet out of you shall come forth to Me the One to be*

Ruler in Israel."

In that moment, boy and herdsman forged a bond of friendship.

What would his parents think, what would Arphaxad think if they heard a shepherd reverently reciting from the sacred scrolls?

"My mother taught the promise to me," Zuar said. His voice broke lightly as he added, "It is because of her that I am this night in Bethlehem."

They approached a turning. Elysmus hesitated.

"What is it?" Zuar inquired.

Elysmus took a further step, the shepherds following.

"That is my father's inn," the boy said, pointing.

The building itself stood dark and silent but on ahead, at the entrance to the stable cave, the Star's light cast an aura of glory as, like a guardian sentinel, the angel appeared . . . the angel who had received the chalice and who had given the innkeeper's son his advent commissioning.

"Come!" the angel called, beaconing.

Any vestige of doubt disappeared from the boy's thinking. Messiah had truly been born this night in Bethlehem. He believed it as surely as any truth known to his young and ardent mind.

Zuar moved quickly ahead, Elysmus following, Enosh and the other two shepherds trailing their footfalls.

"Glory to God in the highest!" sang the Advent Choir. As from a distance, in melodic descant, another sector of voices added, *"On earth peace, good will toward men!"*

"Messiah!" exclaimed Enosh.

"The Promised One!" added Zuar.

When Elysmus and the shepherds reached the cave, the sentinel angel moved between them and the entrance.

"Well done," the angel said to Elysmus.

And the angel was gone.

Zuar became apprehensive. He gestured for Elysmus to lead the way. Elysmus likewise hesitated and the chief of the shepherds touched him with the nub of his staff.

Although descent into the cave was familiar to the boy, he ventured slowly.

"Oh!" all of the group exclaimed as they came into full view of the stable.

"Messiah!" Zuar called out.

Heavenly light encompassed the interior . . . rainbows of color, luminous and yet subdued as one might suppose a throne room to be. All of the hues and tones emerged from the manger area where a babe lay sleeping. The Nazareth carpenter stood watching. The shy mother, as much girl as woman, kept her eyes intent upon the newborn.

The boy's favorite ewe greeted him. He wished to respond but could not poise his lips to speak.

"Come to the Promised One," Joseph said, beckoning.

Elysmus and Zuar took one step of compliance, then stood inert. So overpowering was the spectacle, so aware were they of their unfitness.

"Come," Joseph repeated.

Elysmus and Zuar and the accompanying shepherds proceeded until they came to the manger side. There an unanticipated reality came upon them all. The babe lay tightly wrapped in swaddling bands, motionless, breathing so lightly as to appear mummified in the taut confinement.

Doubt came to Elysmus.

"Is it the Messiah babe?" Zuar asked, his voice quaking with uncertainty.

"The Promised One?" Enosh added.

"The child is like my own firstborn," ventured a third shepherd.

These utterances of uncertainty sent a frightening chill through the boy's body. Was it yet possible he had been mistaken? Could the babe be a prophet given to Israel after the four hundred years of silence?

A prophet?

Not the Messiah?

"O Jehovah!" Elysmus exclaimed. He could think of nothing from the scrolls to comfort or assure him.

But then, as though the very dome of the cave were riven open, the angels resumed their singing!

"Glory to God in the highest and on earth peace, good will toward men!"

In vaulting fortissimo!

In harmonic diminuendo!

In spectacular occurrence, the singing entered slowly into the stable, as though drawn from the skies to now surround the Advent Babe. Loud initially. Deafening. Then, suddenly, the music became a part of everyone's being . . . inner . . . permeating . . . but now soft and assuring, a true Gloria.

"O Jehovah," Elysmus again exclaimed.

"He is very man," said the chief of the shepherds. "He is very God."

Weeping, Zuar dropped to his knees, Elysmus at his side.

The others joined them.

"He is truly Messiah?" asked Enosh.

"Messiah," Zuar responded like a father teaching his son. "The truth is in our hearts!"

Enosh pondered for a long moment before saying. "The truth is in my heart!"

Now the angel voices rose once again in exterior crescendo and the colors in the stable gave precedence to a brilliant shaft of light coming through the entranceway.

Promises from the scrolls of Isaiah.

The prophecy of Micah.

The songs of David.

The counsels of Solomon.

These and the boy's many other learnings at the synagogue became one in an ethos of fulfilling reality.

"Messiah!" Elysmus exclaimed.

"Messiah!" Zuar and the other shepherds repeated after him. It sounded strange coming from the lips of these hardened men. It sounded beautiful as well.

Elysmus thought of Arphaxad.

He thought of his parents.

He thought of the many who had ridiculed his efforts to make known the Advent Truth.

Why did they sleep at such an hour?

He sobbed in anguished regret. Except for Zuar and the lesser shepherds, he had failed the angel's command.

Zuar's burly arm came gently across the boy's slight shoulders. Elysmus looked up at the man who had so frightened him. Zuar's countenance was quiet and assured. He was a man at fullest peace.

Elysmus thought once again of his mother.

His father.

The people at the town center.

Arphaxad.

"Why do not others come?" he asked. "Why do only *we* find the Messiah child?"

With stark suddenness, silence engulfed the stable. The entire cave reverted to its natural darkness, all except the Promised Child over whom a crest of light hung like a royal canopy.

"Dear boy," Zuar began. Tears coursed down his weathered cheeks. Pleasure and pain in equal measure etched his countenance. He looked down at the Messiah babe, then to Elysmus. "What we behold in this stable," he continued, "all the world shall one day know." He paused briefly. "But perhaps a few . . . a few like us, dear boy . . . perhaps only they will ever see the Light and hear the Song!"

·

He who
carpeted the sky
   with galaxies
who arched
   horizons
      across the atom
whose breath
   is life
whose heart
   is love,
whose word
   is truth,
stepped
 down
   from
    the
     eternal
into
 my
  moment
   to grant me
   immortality!

ka